A Note to Parents and Caregivers:

Read-it! Joke Books are for children who are moving ahead on the amazing road to reading. These fun books support the acquisition and extension of reading skills as well as a love of books.

Published by the same company that produces *Read-it!* Readers, these books introduce the question/answer and dialogue patterns that help children expand their thinking about language structure and book formats.

When sharing joke books with a child, read in short stretches. Pause often to talk about the meaning of the jokes. The question/answer and dialogue formats work well for this purpose and provide an opportunity to talk about the language and meaning of the jokes. Have the child turn the pages and point to the pictures and familiar words. When you read the jokes, have fun creating the voices of characters or emphasizing some important words. Be sure to reread favorite jokes.

There is no right or wrong way to share books with children. Find time to read with your child, and pass on the legacy of literacy.

Adria F. Klein, Ph.D.
Professor Emeritus
California State University
San Bernardino, California

Managing Editors: Bob Temple, Catherine Neitge
Creative Director: Terri Foley
Editors: Jerry Ruff, Christianne Jones
Designer: Les Tranby
Page production: Picture Window Books
The illustrations in this book were rendered digitally.

Picture Window Books
5115 Excelsior Boulevard
Suite 232
Minneapolis, MN 55416
877-845-8392
www.picturewindowbooks.com

Printed in the United States of America.

Library of Congress Cataloging-in-Publication Data
Dahl, Michael.
Sit! Stay! Laugh! : a book of pet jokes / by Michael Dahl ;
illustrated by Anne Haberstroh.
p. cm. — (Read-it! joke books—supercharged!)
ISBN 1-4048-0629-6
1. Pets—Juvenile humor. 2. Wit and humor, Juvenile.
I. Title. II. Series.

PN6231.P42M66 2004
818'.602—dc22   2004007325

Sit!
Stay!
Laugh!

A Book of Pet Jokes

By Michael Dahl • Illustrated by Anne Haberstroh

Reading Advisers:
Adria F. Klein, Ph.D.
Professor Emeritus, California State University
San Bernardino, California

Susan Kesselring, M.A., Literacy Educator
Rosemount-Apple Valley-Eagan (Minnesota) School District

PICTURE WINDOW BOOKS
Minneapolis, Minnesota

How can you tell if
a snake is a baby?

It has a rattle.

What did the dog say when
he sat on sandpaper?

Ruff! Ruff!

Why did the little girl make her
pet chicken sit on the roof?

She liked egg rolls.

What kind of dog likes flowers?

A budhound.

Why do dogs have such big families?

*Because they each
have four paws.*

What kind of dog wears a uniform and a badge?

A guard dog.

Why do baby skunks make the worst pets?

They're always little stinkers.

What do you get when you put a kitten in the photocopy machine?

A copycat.

Where do dogs go when
they lose their tails?

> *A re-tail store.*

What do you get when you cross
a canary with a snake?

> *A sing-a-long.*

What pet comes with its own
mobile home?

> *A turtle.*

Why did the cowboy buy
a dachshund?

> *Everybody told him to
> "get a long, little doggie."*

What type of music do bunnies
play at parties?

> *Hip-hop.*

Why don't dogs make good dancers?

> *Because they have
> two left feet!*

Did you hear about the goldfish
who became a quarterback?

> *He wanted to play in a Super Bowl!*

Why did the puppy bite
the man's ankle?

*Because it couldn't
reach any higher.*

What kind of coat does
a pet dog wear?

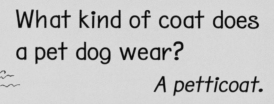

> *A petticoat.*

Why is a group of puppies
called a litter?

> *Because they mess
> up the whole house.*

What do you get if your
cat drinks lemonade?

> *A sourpuss.*

Why did the cat buy
a computer?
>So he could play with
>his very own mouse.

Why did the dog sleep
under the car?
>He wanted to wake up "oily."

How do you spell "mousetrap"
with just three letters?
>C-A-T.

What do you call kittens
that like to bowl?

Alley cats.

What do you call young dogs
that play in the snow?

Slush puppies.

What did the hungry dalmatian
say after a meal?

"That hit the spots!"

How many pet skunks do you have?

Quite a phew!

What do you give a pet rabbit
for dessert?

A hopsicle.

13

What kind of dog can cook
dinner for its owner?

An oven mutt.

What is a polygon?
*When your pet parrot
flies out of its cage.*

Why did the kitten put the letter
M into the freezer?

*To turn some "ice"
into "mice."*

What did the girl do when she found her pet dog eating the dictionary?

She took the words right out of his mouth.

What kind of dog is like a short skirt?

A peekin' knees.

What pet fish are the most expensive?

Goldfish.

Why did the boy take a bag of oats to bed?

To feed his night-mare.

What kind of beds do fish sleep on?

Waterbeds.

What do you call a koala without any socks on?

Bearfoot.

What does a dog put in his house?

Fur-niture.

How did the girl talk
to her pet fish?

She dropped it a line.

How can you tell that carrots
are good for your eyes?

> *Because rabbits never
> wear glasses.*

What do you give a dog with
a fever?

> *Mustard. It's the best
> thing for a hot dog.*

Why are some fish found at the
bottom of the ocean?

> *Because they dropped
> out of school.*

What do you get when you cross
an elephant with a goldfish?

Swimming trunks.

What do frogs like to drink in
the winter?

Hot croako.

What do you call a dog that just
made a hole in the front yard?

Doug.

19

Why are mice so noisy
after they take a bath?

They're squeaky clean.

Where do you leave your dog
when you go shopping?

In the barking lot.

What is small, furry, and smells
like bacon?

A ham-ster.

What cats purr more than
any other?

Purr-sians.

What kind of dog likes to
answer the telephone?

A golden receiver.

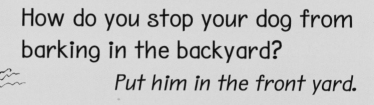

How do you stop your dog from
barking in the backyard?

Put him in the front yard.

Where do young dogs sleep
when they go camping?

Pup tents.

What do cats drink on hot
summer days?

Miced tea.

Which side of a cat has the most fur?

> *The outside!*

What did the dog say about his day in the woods?

> *Bark, bark, bark, bark. . . .*

What do dogs like to eat for breakfast?

> *Pooched eggs.*

Look for all of the books in this series:

Read-it! Joke Books—Supercharged!

Beastly Laughs
A Book of Monster Jokes

Chalkboard Chuckles
A Book of Classroom Jokes

Creepy Crawlers
A Book of Bug Jokes

Roaring with Laughter
A Book of Animal Jokes

Sit! Stay! Laugh!
A Book of Pet Jokes

Spooky Sillies
A Book of Ghost Jokes

Read-it! Joke Books

Alphabet Soup
A Book of Riddles About Letters

Animal Quack-Ups
Foolish and Funny Jokes About Animals

Bell Buzzers
A Book of Knock-Knock Jokes

Chewy Chuckles
Deliciously Funny Jokes About Food

Crazy Criss-Cross
A Book of Mixed-Up Riddles

Ding Dong
A Book of Knock-Knock Jokes

Dino Rib Ticklers
Hugely Funny Jokes About Dinosaurs

Doctor, Doctor
A Book of Doctor Jokes

Door Knockers
A Book of Knock-Knock Jokes

Family Funnies
A Book of Family Jokes

Funny Talk
A Book of Silly Riddles

Galactic Giggles
Far-Out and Funny Jokes About Outer Space

Laughs on a Leash
A Book of Pet Jokes

Monster Laughs
Frightfully Funny Jokes About Monsters

Nutty Neighbors
A Book of Knock-Knock Jokes

Open Up and Laugh!
A Book of Knock-Knock Jokes

Rhyme Time
A Book of Rhyming Riddles

School Buzz
Classy and Funny Jokes About School

School Daze
A Book of Riddles About School

Teacher Says
A Book of Teacher Jokes

Three-Alarm Jokes
A Book of Firefighter Jokes

Under Arrest
A Book of Police Jokes

Who's There?
A Book of Knock-Knock Jokes

Zoodles
A Book of Riddles About Animals